D1275464

For Nicole — for doing this!
— R.H.H.

For my cats, who have to put up with a lot.
— N.H.

The illustrator wishes to acknowledge
Evan Sult, her production consultant.

Text copyright © 2005 by Bee Productions, Inc.
Illustrations copyright © 2005 by Nicole Hollander

Little, Brown and Company

Time Warner Book Group
1271 Avenue of the Americas, New York, NY 10020
Visit our Web site at www.lb-kids.com

First Edition

Library of Congress Cataloging-in-Publication Data

Harris, Robie H.
 I'm so mad! / by Robie Harris ; illustrated by Nicole Hollander. — 1st ed.
   p. cm. — (Just being me)
  Summary: A little girl and her mother enjoy shopping at the grocery store until the girl has a tantrum when her mother will not buy ice cream. Includes brief notes on handling a child's tantrums.
 ISBN 0-316-10939-8
[1. Behavior — Fiction. 2. Temper tantrums — Fiction. 3. Anger — Fiction. 4. Shopping — Fiction. 5. Mother and child — Fiction.] I. Title: I am so mad!. II. Hollander, Nicole, ill. III. Title.
PZ7.H2436Iabg 2005
[E]–dc22
                                                                    2004013948

10 9 8 7 6 5 4 3 2 1

IM

Printed in China

The illustrations for this book were done in pen and ink. Color was added using Adobe Photoshop.
The text was set in Providence and Sylvia (designed by Nicole Hollander and Tom Greensfelder),
and the display type is Drunk Cyrillic.

I'm SO Mad!

By Robie H. Harris
Illustrated by Nicole Hollander

LITTLE, BROWN AND COMPANY
New York ∽ Boston

Today, when Mommy and I went shopping, Mommy said I could get a flower.

I picked out a pretty yellow one.

I love going shopping with Mommy!

Then Mommy said I could get any kind of bread.
I picked the fattest loaf—and hugged it tight!

"Squished bread... squashed toast!" Mommy groaned.
"Squish-squashed!" I sang. "Squish-squashed!"

When we walked by the freezer,
Mommy took a bag of peas.

I grabbed a box of ice-cream sandwiches.

"Sweetie, it's too early for ice cream," said Mommy.

"Please," I said. "Pretty please? I love ice cream!"

We don't
need
ice cream.

But I
even said
"PLEASE"!

"Please put it back," said Mommy. "We have ice cream at home." I hugged the box tight.

Mommy took the box and put it back.
I didn't like that one bit.

"But Mommy!" I said. "You love ice cream too!
And I want ice cream NOW!"
"Not now!" Mommy said.
And she picked me up and plunked me in the cart.

NOW—I didn't like MOMMY one bit!

And I made a big fuss. A REALLY big, NOISY fuss!

NO, NO-OOOOO, MOMMY!

I WANT OUT, MOMMY! Get me OOOOO-OUT!

Mommy pushed the cart past a giant pyramid of oranges.
Mommy was mad too. But Mommy LOVES oranges.
"Oranges, Mommy!" I whispered. "So many oranges!"

Mommy stopped.

"You can take an orange," she said.
 So I took one.

and rolled —

all over the floor.

"Look what I did, Mommy!" I said.
Then I laughed a tiny laugh.
Mommy didn't laugh.

OH MY! —

"Look what you did!" said Mommy.
Then she smiled a tiny smile.

Mommy lifted me out of the cart.
We piled a gazillion oranges
one by one —
and very carefully —
back onto the table.

I put two oranges in the shopping cart.
Mommy said that was okay and gave me a big hug.
I gave Mommy an even bigger hug.

I Love you —
ANd ORANGes
    too!

I LOVE you,
AND ice
CREAM too!

"NOW," said Mommy,
"let's go home for lunch!"

After lunch, we both ate an orange.
Oranges are yummy!

The next afternoon when we went shopping,
Mommy said, "Today, let's get some ice cream."
And we did!

What's Going On?

For a young child, a trip to the store can be a special time to be with Mommy or Daddy, to explore and to share discoveries with a parent. In this story, the mother makes the trip truly a shared adventure by letting her daughter choose which kind of flower and bread to buy. When the child hugs and squishes the bread, this mother turns "squish-squash" into a game, making it a part of having a good time together. But almost every store is a vast, undiscovered country for a young child, full of wonders at every turn. There are so many exciting possibilities that sometimes children can feel overwhelmed and can become overexcited and irritable.

No matter what, it's often impossible to avoid the moment when a child reaches for the most tempting thing—and wants it *now*. For young children, "now" is the word of the day, and waiting is a virtue learned only over time. When a parent says "no" or "not now," the result can be an inconsolable child and a potentially difficult moment for the parent. But once the parent takes a deep breath and realizes that the tantrum will soon be over, and that the task at hand will take longer than expected, he or she can help the child move on. The mother in this story allows her daughter to take an orange, and then when they tumble, instead of getting angry or frustrated, she laughs with her child. When parents can find such ways to show their children that they understand and accept their strong feelings, then what could have been a disastrous shopping outing becomes an adventure that they can laugh about together. Children learn, too, that becoming angry at a parent every now and then is a natural and accepted part of a loving relationship.

-Linda C. Mayes, MD

Arnold Gesell Professor of Child Psychiatry, Pediatrics, and Psychology at the Yale University Child Study Center and Chairman of the Directorial Team of the Anna Freud Centre, London